Copyright © 2001 by Nord-Süd Verlag AG, Gossau Zürich, Switzerland
First published in Switzerland under the title *Die Drei Kleinen Kaninchen*
English translation copyright © 2002 by North-South Books, Inc.

First published in the United States, Great Britain, Canada, Australia, and New Zealand in 2002
by North-South Books, an imprint of Nord-Süd Verlag AG, Gossau Zürich, Switzerland
Distributed in the United States by North-South Books Inc., New York

Library of Congress Cataloging-in-Publication Data is available.
The CIP catalogue record for this book is available from The British Library.

ISBN 0-7358-1474-0 (trade) 10 9 8 7 6 5 4 3 2 1
ISBN 0-7358-1475-9 (library) 10 9 8 7 6 5 4 3 2 1
Printed in Italy

For more information about our books, and the authors and artists
who create them, visit our web site: www.northsouth.com

A MICHAEL NEUGEBAUER BOOK
NORTH-SOUTH BOOKS / NEW YORK / LONDON

THE THREE LITTLE RABBITS

A Balkan Folktale
Retold and Illustrated by Ivan Gantschev
Translated by J. Alison James

Once upon a time there were three little rabbits. They lived with their mother and their father in a snug burrow in the ground.
One day the father called to his children. "You are now grown up," he said. "It is time that you go and see the wide world. But first dig yourself a safe rabbit hole. And if a fox comes around . . ."
"We must hide in the ground!" cried the three little rabbits.

The three little rabbits said good-bye and hopped out
into the wide world.
They were proud and excited. At last they were grown up!
They no longer had to do everything they were told.
They were free to do what they pleased.

The first rabbit found a lovely place for his home.
"I don't have to do what I am told. So I don't have to dig a hole," he said.
"I'll just make myself a soft nest."
He gathered up branches, hay, and moss. Soon his nest was finished,
and the rabbit had lots of time to eat and play.

The rabbit hopped out to the meadow and nibbled some tender shoots. He sniffed something. It was the fox, lurking nearby. A hungry fox who wanted to catch a little rabbit.

If the fox is around, I must hide in the ground, thought the little rabbit. But all he had was his nest. A nest is for the birds; it is no place for a rabbit to hide.

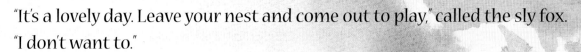

"It's a lovely day. Leave your nest and come out to play," called the sly fox.
"I don't want to."
"THEN I'LL GET YOU!"
The fox pounced with a bound. He snarled and scrabbled and sniffed all around.
Blast it, where was that rabbit?

The second rabbit, too, had found a fine place to live.
"A hole takes too long. I think I'll build myself a hut.
Then I'll be free to do as I please!" said the little rabbit.
He gathered branches, moss, and leaves. Soon his new house
was finished, and the little rabbit had time to eat and play.
He hopped happily out to the meadow.

After a while the little rabbit sniffed something.
It was the fox, skulking nearby. A hungrier fox who
wanted to catch this little rabbit.
    If a fox is around, I must hide in the ground,
    thought the little rabbit.
        But all he had was his hut, and a stick house
        is no place for a rabbit to hide.

"It's a lovely day. Come out to play," called the sly fox.
"I don't want to."
"THEN I'LL GET YOU!"
The fox pounced with a bound. He snarled and scrabbled
and sniffed and snarled and scrabbled and sniffed all around.
Blast it, where was that rabbit?

The third rabbit knew right away where she wanted to live. "Here I'll dig myself a deep, snug burrow," she said. "And when I am finished, I will be free to do what I please." She dug all night and dug all day. She had no time to eat or play. Finally she gathered grass and hay and made herself a soft bed deep under the ground. At last her burrow was finished. She squeezed up through the entrance hole and went out to the meadow. Happily she romped around, played in the sun, and ate everything that tasted good: sorrel, clover, and roots. But then she sniffed the fox prowling about. He was hungrier than ever.

If a fox is around, I must hide in the ground, thought the little rabbit, and she slipped into her burrow. The rabbit hole was a perfect place to hide!

"It's a lovely day. Leave your hole and come out to play," growled the hungry fox.
"CATCH ME IF YOU CAN!" laughed the little rabbit.
The fox pounced with a bound. He snarled and scrabbled and sniffed and snarled and scrabbled and sniffed. . . . But no matter how much he snarled and scrabbled and sniffed, he couldn't reach the little rabbit!

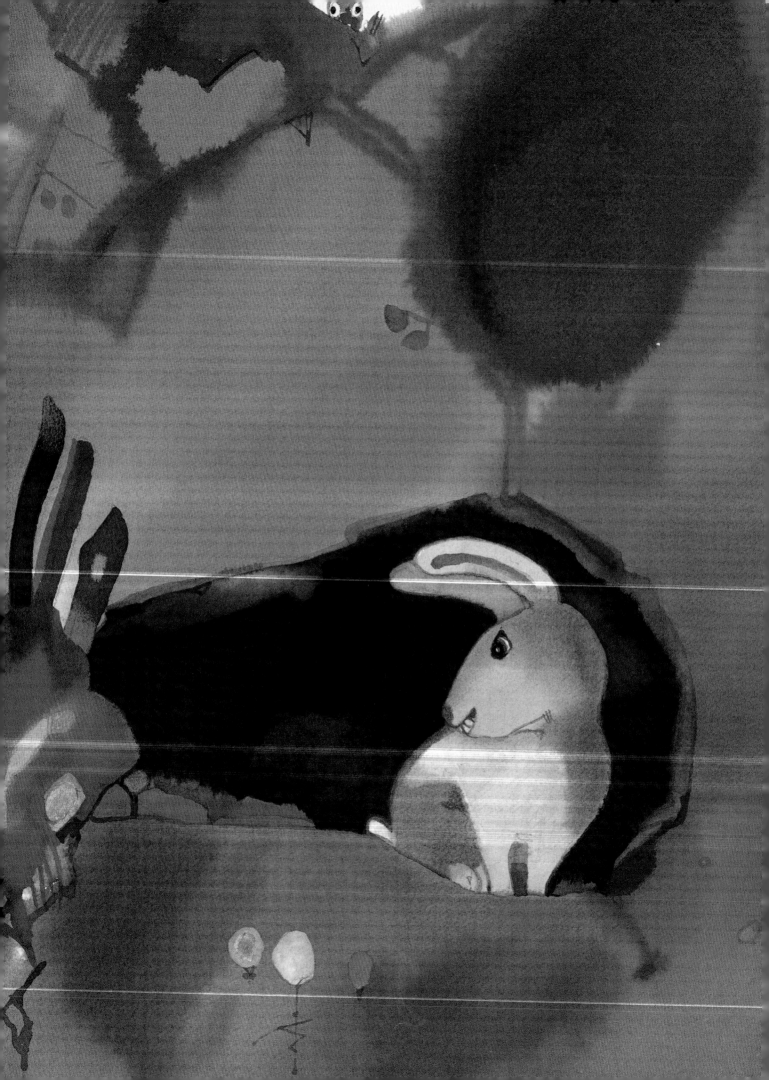

The hole was narrow, and with all that scrabbling, the fox got his head stuck tight. He wriggled and jiggled, but he could not go in and could not get out.

Help me, please!" cried the fox in desperation.

Oh, dear," said the little rabbit cheerfully. "I am big now and I do not have to do what I'm told. I can do whatever I please. And I'm not sure that I want to help you. You were going to eat me."

Please, please," howled the fox. "I'll give you anything, anything that you want!"

Then give me your word that you will leave me and my brothers in peace!" demanded the rabbit.

Ow, Ow! I promise," yowled the fox. "All right, I will! Just help me out of here!"

The rabbit gave the fox such a shove on the nose that he tumbled over backwards, right out of the hole.
With dirty fur and a hungry belly, the fox slunk away.

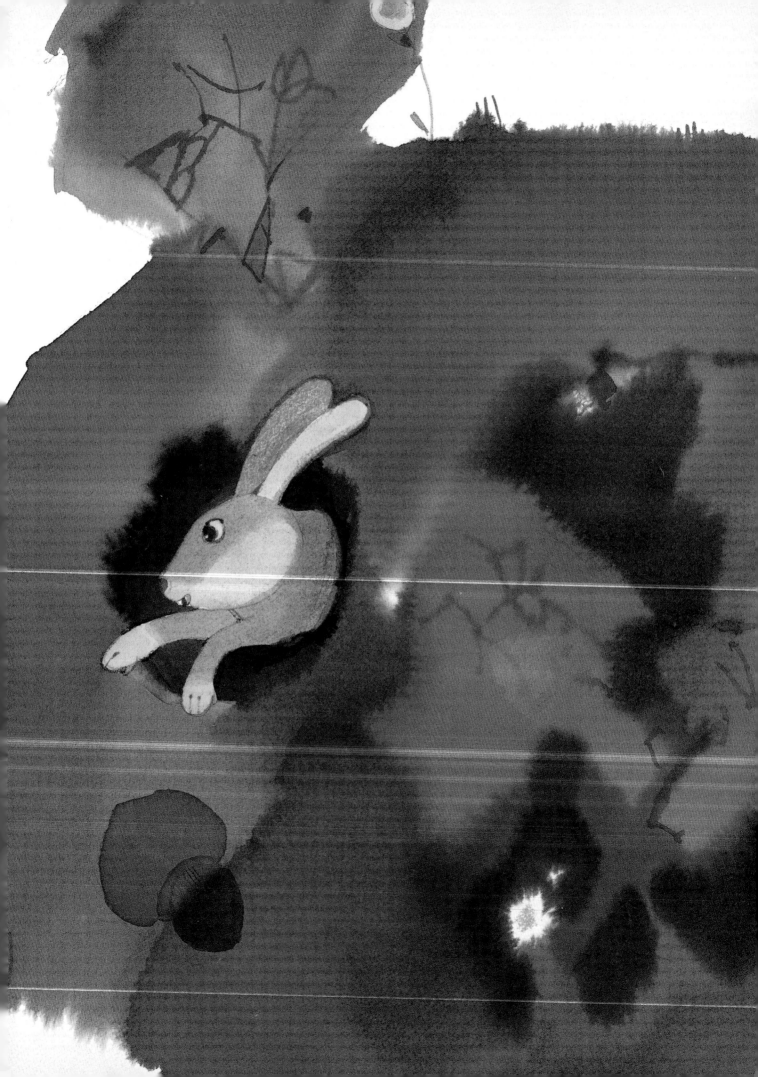

The first two rabbits now took the time to dig their own safe, warm burrows.
When that job was done, the three little rabbits ran to the meadow to play and eat whatever they pleased.
But a fox is a fox after all, and when he forgot his promise and came sniffing around . . .

They hid in their holes in the ground!

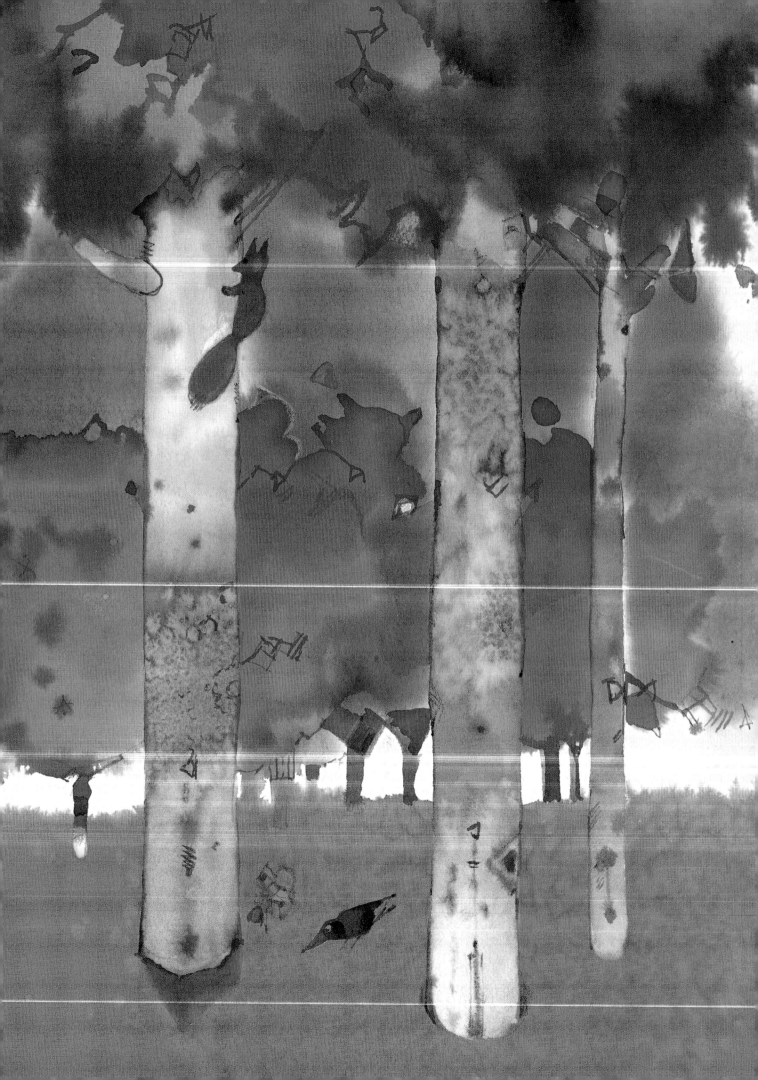